BENEATH SHIVERING SKIES

Beneath Shivering Skies

DARK FOLKLORE

Georgina Jeffery

Coblyn Press

Contents

Fledgling

Yolanthe is smiling at me.

She has often smiled at me, in passing, in brief flashes, hidden under the shadow of her ice cream stand's canopy. Just as another customer, passing through her sunny square, stopping to lurk by the picnic tables and overflowing bins. Except I have never been a customer, never bought an ice cream from beautiful Yolanthe.

It is a quiet day; there is no queue to her stall. She wears orange shorts high up on her thighs and a matching cropped blouse that reveals a band of midriff beneath her apron. The sun's warm rays wash over the rich ochre glow of her skin.

She has noticed me noticing her smiling. She ducks her head a moment, and I'm sorry to see the smile leave. Then her eyes flick furtively back to mine, and I feel a little sick with the stir of a nervous bird flapping about in my chest. I have never spoken to Yolanthe. I am not supposed to speak to Yolanthe.

My feet tip-toe to her stand. Her cheeks tinge pink, but she is smiling again.

'Hello,' she says, tucking tightly woven black braids behind one ear.

I nod, uncertain. Her smile falters.

'I'm Yolanthe,' she says.

'I know,' I reply. She seems taken aback. I rush to explain myself. 'I've heard people say your name.'

There is something playful in the twist of her mouth. 'You've been paying such close attention to me?'

I'm not sure how to answer, except with the truth. 'Yes.'

She gives a sharp intake of breath. She was not expecting this reply.

'I– I see you in the square a lot,' she says, stumbling over the words. She fidgets with one braid over her shoulder. 'You're here every Saturday, at least. Do you live in town?'

'No.'

'You come in for school?'

'No.'

'Oh . . .' She seems puzzled, until her gaze lights up again. 'Do you work nearby? I wondered if you were older than me.'

I hesitate. I've clearly not met her expectations, and I fear losing the thread of our conversation if I don't meet another. I test the feel of the lie on my tongue. 'Y-es.'

'I'm eighteen,' she says quickly, with a blush deepening over her cheekbones. 'I'm in my last year of school. Saving up to move out next year, maybe.' She gestures to the glistening trays of ice cream. 'What do you do?'

In the satchel slung over my dress, the weight of a handful of peaches inspires my answer. 'I . . . pick fruit.'

'Is it fun?'

My thoughts become a confused squall as I struggle to decipher this question. 'It's . . . peaches.'

Yolanthe laughs, a light titter that dances in the air between us. 'I'll bet it's more fun than ice cream. I'm stuck in the same spot all day. I'd rather be moving around.' While speaking, she selects a cone and draws her scoop through a carton of pale, creamy gelato. She holds the ice cream out to me with a grin. 'Peach.'

'I don't have any money,' I start, panicked. But Yolanthe tuts and shushes me, pressing the cone into my hand.

'Relax. Let's call it a free sample. So that you'll come back for more.' She doesn't look at me as she says this. But when her eyes slide back to mine, I feel like she is trying to ask another question – one I can't easily translate.

Ice cream is dripping onto my fingers. I taste it, and flinch as the cold hits my tongue. It is the sweetest, coldest thing I have ever eaten. I'm not sure I like it.

Yolanthe watches me with interest. The weight of her gaze is heavy; it feels as though everyone in the square is looking at me. I am agonisingly aware of every tiny movement of my tongue as it laps at the cold dessert. I hope I'm not doing it wrong.

More than a minute of silence passes while I focus on this monumental task, growing ever more anxious as the ice cream slowly disappears. Anxiety is rolling off Yolanthe as well: she twists her braids in her hands, staring at the ground.

Maybe I am supposed to have left? Is she waiting for me to leave?

But just as my lungs clench with this fear, Yolanthe blurts out another question.

'Where do you live?' she asks. Her wide eyes betray her embarrassment. 'If you don't mind me asking.'

I do mind. But she did gift me the ice cream, so I grasp for a sensible scrap of information to impart in return. 'I live with my mother. Outside of town. It's a long way.' I bite the inside of my cheek. This feels like too much to reveal.

But Yolanthe thinks nothing of it. 'I'd like to live far out in the countryside. I hike in the mountains sometimes. Do you like to hike?'

I have never thought about whether I liked it. It is something I have always had to do. 'Yes,' I reply carefully.

She bounces on the balls of her feet. There is nervous energy behind her next words as they spill out on top of each other. 'We should go together sometime. You could show me some trails around where you live.'

I picture Yolanthe striding up my mountain-side under the golden sun. Bare shoulders revealed where her blouse flaps open in the breeze. A shiver rushes up my spine. 'I need to head home.'

'Oh.' A flash of panic across her face. 'Can I ... What's your name?'

'Iphis.' I try for a smile, hope it doesn't come off as a snarl.

She returns it, brightly. 'That sounds pretty.'

I feel heat creeping up my neck. No one has ever told me my name sounds pretty before.

'Will you be back?' she asks. 'Same time next week?'

'Yes.'

I turn to go, realise too late that my departure was hasty as I leave her trailing a farewell behind me.

'See you ... See you, then ... Iphis.' Then I hear her muttering to herself. 'Stupid. *Let's go hiking!* What a stupid thing to suggest, Yolanthe ...'

I finish the wafer cone and lick the last of the cream from my fingers. It is probably the best food I will eat today. I try to put Yolanthe out of my mind.

I tighten my grip on my satchel and weave through the near-empty streets. Haze rises from the cobblestones. It is a dry, baking heat, and no one is doing good business today. The restaurants are throwing out wasted food, but it is rotting before I can steal it from their bins. Grilled fish turns putrid under the harsh sun; salad leaves shrivel in brown slime.

Earlier I found someone had left cherry tomatoes drying on a slab outside their house, and scooped the whole clutch into my bag. A poke into residential dustbins yielded better treasures: a handful of batteries, a sturdy plastic water bottle, an assortment of newspapers.

I sidle into the small pharmacy I haven't visited in a while. Drop my head, let my hair hide my face as I sneak into the feminine products aisle. I think the cashier has spotted me: a dumpy, middle-aged woman, I know she won't be able to catch me. I snag two packets of sanitary towels and head for the door.

'Hey!' the woman shouts, scrambling to exit her counter. 'Wait there!'

I bolt. I am at the end of the street before she is even out of the door, and I am certain she will not follow as I turn the corner. Still, I do not stop running until I am near the edge of the town, and the land opens up to greet me.

I am hiking, I reflect, as I plod along the uneven dirt trails. Sheep look up from their grazing to track my passage. I stop at a spring to fill my new water bottle and top up the others in my pack.

Soon I leave the marked path and make my own way across the slopes. It takes me several hours. I do not know the name of my mountain, if it has one, nor the name of the secluded gorge, hidden by trees, where the entrance to my home lies.

The sun is behind the peaks by the time I reach it. I scramble to an overhanging rock which shelters a hollow basin in the earth. Sliding into it, branches crack under my arrival to the nest. I am getting too heavy for its delicate construction.

'I'm home, Mum,' I call softly into the darkness.

Feathers rustle in response. Her talons stretch out from under one iridescent wing. In the mass of black feathers a yellow eye opens.

'Isssss foooood?' she asks.

'Some.' I empty my satchel, displaying the stolen tomatoes, four fresh-plucked peaches, and a carton of nuts someone had thrown out for being past its sell-by-date. 'Slim pickings, today.'

'You were carefuuuuul?'

'I didn't spend long in the town,' I reply. I avoid

the thought that I'd wasted precious time talking to Yolanthe.

Mum nods. She impales a peach with one talon and drags it to her mouth. Behind her rosy lips are hidden sharp teeth that rip into the fleshy pulp. Her other foot extends, clutching something small and bloody. She releases the rabbit carcass and allows me to pick it up.

I grab my serrated knife and begin to skin the animal. The pelt is soft on my fingertips; the exposed muscle slick beneath. I cut the meat into thin strips and divide the pile in half between us.

Mum snatches the meat to her mouth. I pour water over mine, washing away the blood. My teeth don't tear the lean flesh as easily as Mum's. I spend more time chewing, while she gulps large pieces down whole. I would normally build a fire to cook, but I'm down to my last few matches, and besides – Mum doesn't like the flames.

In many ways, there is little similarity between us. If not for the vibrance of her eagle-gold eyes, her face alone could be mistaken for human. Her long hair is darker than mine, her lips fuller, cheekbones higher. From the chest down any shared resemblance to my body ends.

The feathers bristle on her long neck as she rears her head. She yawns loudly, stretching her human vocal chords. Finding the rhythm between syllables.

'We musssssst move soon,' she says.

My heart sinks. 'Already? I don't think anyone knows my face in town yet.' *Except Yolanthe.* 'We could stay a few more weeks. I'll wait longer before my next trip.'

'Noooo. Danger.'

I look around sadly at the trimmings of our nest. It took me a whole month to scavenge the pretty things that make it feel like home. Fairy lights, in the shape of plastic daisies, are strung around the edges. Soft blankets, padded with mother's feathers, make up a cosy bed in one corner, and I'd found a discarded teddy bear, with one eye missing and left foot bursting open with white fluff, to garnish it. My favourite pillow, a shimmering treasure covered in sequins, had taken me a whole week to wash out the garbage grime until it sparkled gold and pink once again.

We shall have to leave them all behind when we move. I'm growing too heavy for Mum to carry. My bones are not filled with air like hers.

I wipe my bloody hands on a rag. Reach for the fairy lights and the newly scavenged batteries. One by one, I try them in the plastic casing. 'Okay, Mum. I understand. I'll do one last trip in a couple of days, and then we shall go.'

'No.'

I stall in my task. 'But the moonless sky isn't for another week! I can get another hunt in before then.'

Mum shakes her head from side to side. She is unsettled. 'You sssstay in the nest.'

I throw down the fairy lights. 'No one knows we're here! The nearest shepherds are still miles away. And I've never even seen another person on the trails leading through our hills–'

'Not aaaaall dangersss are human,' she says, cutting me off.

I tense. 'Wolves?' I whisper. 'A bear?'

Mum chitters, a troubled sound. 'Sssstay in the nest.'

Glumly, I concede. 'Yes, Mum.'

She turns to preening her feathers while I pick up the batteries again. Finally, I find two that cause the lights to flare back to life. I hang them up again, and spend some time staring at their loveliness in the darkness of our nest.

As the night draws in, I burrow into my blankets and pull out my wind-up radio, the only treasure Mum will allow me to bring along with each relocation. Mum cocks her head as I wind it, eyes narrowing at the blare of static when I switch it on. The buzzing of it disorients her. But she creeps next to me once I've tuned to the local radio station, and for the next hour we listen in on the weather reports and recent news.

Someone is complaining of animals eating the crops in their orchard. There are reports of missing sheep from the next valley over: Mum's traces, and the reason we are keeping to small game like rabbits and birds for a while.

I wish to point out that there is no news of a thief in the town, nor sightings of a wild child roaming the hills.

But there is part of me that wishes there were a small thing, an indication I had been seen, noticed. I remember Yolanthe's smile and guiltily clutch it to my chest. I dream up radio headlines for us: *Today, Iphis spoke to Yolanthe. The weather is set to remain warm, with Yolanthe's legs crossed over one another while she rides in on an encroaching heatwave. Her smile is forecast to be bright and sunny for the next week. Beware rainfall after the new moon. Bring an umbrella. The clouds will turn grey.*

The news is followed by music, and Mum loses interest. I lower the volume and bop my head to the tinny, synthetic sounds, like I've seen other people do. I wonder whether Yolanthe likes this music, if she might be listening to the same radio station, and the thought warms me.

Mum nudges my arm. It is time to sleep. I switch off the radio and the fairy lights. A narrow oval of starlight becomes the only illumination in the darkness. Mum folds me into her embrace. I cuddle into the warmth of her breasts while she wraps black wings around me.

The lights go out.

First Flight

I cannot stand the monotony of the nest. It is two days from new moon, the night where the least light shines in the sky and we can be safest in making a long journey. I measure the shrinking slivers of moon against my thumbnail, as if I am carving them away each night.

Yolanthe sees this moon, I think. We are both under it, together.

It is cruel that I'm not allowed to see her again. Our thread of connection was so fine, barely a hair's breadth of association. But she'd wanted to go hiking with me, and she talked as though we could be friends, and as though a hair could be spun into a strong cord between us.

Will you be back? she'd asked me.

I wind and rewind my radio, and don't really

listen as I stare at the thick woven walls of our nest. Mum hunts throughout the night, returns in early dawn gloom.

We eat her meagre catch, a handful of sparrows and two small fish. She seems to be extra cautious lately, not daring to travel far or hunt larger prey.

While she preens, I burrow deep into my heap of blankets and pretend to sleep. I feel her poke about the pile, seeking to envelop me in her hold. Her bony arms curl round my foetal form, hidden by many layers, and her wings drape loosely to the sides.

Soon she sleeps, with quick and shallow breaths.

I wait until I can see the sun peeking into our hole. She sleeps most deeply in the daylight. Then I begin to wriggle out of my fluffy mound. Mum shifts – her clawed hands clutch briefly at the blankets, then relax – and I am free.

I hesitate, staring at her peaceful, vulnerable shape in the middle of our nest. Her skin, where it shows, is pale, white as the moon. Her face, at rest, is very beautiful, though her cheeks are sallow. She looks thin. Hungry. I vow to return with food.

Perhaps, then, she will forgive me.

I leap lightly from the nest, picking my way carefully down the slopes and through the trees.

Some concerns flutter about my head. My clothes are more soiled than they would usually be for a town hunt. I notice how clean other people keep themselves; it is not something the pecking of my mother nor my own talentless preening can achieve. So I would normally bathe and wash my clothes in the river, before entering a large place where people gather.

I stop by a stream and run my hair through its clear waters. It is cool and pure. I strip off my tunic dress, which is beginning to become small for me – I'd have liked to steal another before moving on. A quick rinse to rid the sweat from my skin, and a self-conscious scrub at the mud patches on the dress. There are enough hours for it to dry in the sun as I walk.

I continue my journey, damp and fresh.

At a quick pace, it takes around half a day to reach the town. The land wakes up around me; birds take to the sky and animals leave their burrows. The cobbles are hot by the time I breach the town walls. When I enter the square, the sun is peaking in the sky and Yolanthe is in her usual lunchtime spot.

A man is buying an ice cream for his child at her stall. Yolanthe catches my eye, mid-scoop.

She looks away quickly, as if to hide the sly up-turning of her mouth. The man hands her bright coins that shine in the sun. His daughter squeals with delight at the dripping gelato in its sweet waffle cone. I wait until they are across the square before I approach Yolanthe.

'Back again?' she says, with a twinkle of humour.

'I wouldn't miss it . . .' I reply, not fully under-standing what it was I might have missed. Something about this moment. An unspoken promise, from our last meeting. The stirrings of a future I could never hope to entertain – and yet I also couldn't let it collapse without a final word. This is what drove me to escape the nest today.

'I'm leaving,' I burst out. 'I won't be able to see you again.'

Yolanthe's face screws into confusion. 'Moving away? So suddenly?'

'It's my mother's decision.'

She frowns, a spark of surrogate indignation lighting up her dark eyes. 'Do *you* want to go?'

'I . . .' The question stuns me. 'It's not up to me.'

'Rubbish,' she scoffs. 'She can't make you. Can you afford to move out?' She glances down to the colourful tubs, chewing her bottom lip. 'Nico's looking for someone to pick up extra weekend hours at the stall. I could put in a good word. If you wanted.'

In less than a second, an entire lifetime of possibilities burns through my brain. Iphis, the good daughter, running away from Mum. Iphis and Yolanthe, slinging ice cream together, giggling under the sun. Money jingling in my pockets instead of half-worn batteries. Ordering food from the little blue café, instead of going through its bins. Iphis and Yolanthe, building a nest together, the human kind with pretty white walls and soft cushions in every room.

My heart quivers with longing. Mum would never allow it.

'My mother . . .' I trail off with a sigh.

'Can't you talk to her?' Yolanthe says, undeterred. 'Persuade her?'

'She wouldn't even approve of me being here.'

'Then why did you come today?' She raises an eyebrow, crosses her arms over her chest.

I hang my head. 'I came to say goodbye.'

'No, you didn't.'

Yolanthe tosses back her hair and leans toward me, forcing me to meet to her gaze. To witness the intensity of it. She is not smiling now. I realise I am staring at her lips. Her eyes drop to mine in mirror movement.

'Ladies.'

An old man smiles at us, not comprehending what precipice he might have pulled us back from. Yolanthe grips her scoop too tightly.

'What can I get you?' she asks. The old man gives his order, and she fills a cone with strawberry gelato. As she hands him his change she says to me curtly, 'Weren't you leaving?'

I recognise an edge in her voice, like a warning flex of talons. She is not happy with me. Perhaps she did not like the way I looked at her.

I watch the old man shuffle away. I'm afraid to look at Yolanthe again. 'I'm sorry. I don't know what I hoped to achieve by coming here. Maybe I wanted to pretend I could have what isn't possible. Thank you for talking to me, Yolanthe.'

I turn and pace across the square. I imagine Yolanthe watching me walk away with indifference. It causes cold fire to burn in my chest, along with a prickle of tears behind my eyes.

Suddenly, footsteps. I tense at their speed, chasing up to me. A warm hand lands on my shoulder and I whirl, ready to either fight or run depending on my attacker. But it is Yolanthe who meets my startled gaze.

There is panic in her eyes. Ice cream drips from the scoop onto her apron.

'Can you . . .' Her grip tenses: some resolve in her tightens. 'Can you meet me? In an hour? By the old orchard on the edge of town?'

My gut twists. The sun is already high in the sky. I intended to get back to the nest before sunset. I don't wish to risk Mum finding out I'd disobeyed.

'Yes,' I breathe.

She nods, flits back to her stall like a frightened bird. This time when I imagine her watching me walk away, it is with a great swell of excitement trembling under my skin.

I skirt around the most familiar streets – avoiding the pharmacy, the blue café and its bins – and make my way straight to the orchard. It lies beyond a crumbling dry-stone wall, in a tangle of weeds and climbing vines that shroud the trees. Perhaps the orchard was once well-cared for, but now it gives a sense of frailty. The boughs hang low, as though drained of strength, while mounds of unpicked fruit rot on the ground.

I root around for some fresh pickings, but it is too late in the season and most of the fruit has decayed too far. The sweet-vinegar scent of fermentation surrounds me while I wait. I fret with my hair, comb fingers through the fine strands; contemplate twisting it into tight braids like Yolanthe's. My efforts produce only tangles. In the end I leave it hanging loosely down my back.

Time stretches. The sun passes its zenith and starts the downward descent. My eyes measure the lengths of shadows. I begin to think Yolanthe isn't coming.

Why should she?

Yolanthe has a family, and work that brings her money, and she can pay for food and soft things in the town. I am a scavenger on the fringe of her territory, picking up the pieces that overflow, that will not be missed. Even Yolanthe's attention: I seem to have scrounged it out of nothing. And I've nothing to offer in return.

She is not coming, and I will not make it home on time.

I've turned towards the hills when I hear frantic footsteps behind me. I crouch behind a tree, take account of the heavy panting. A voice calls out quietly, as though afraid to shout beyond a whisper, 'Iphis?'

I rise from my hiding place, stepping into view. Yolanthe's cheeks are flushed, her breathing rapid – she looks as though she has run all the way here. She is still wearing her apron, perhaps forgot to take it off in the rush. She speaks first.

'I– I'm sorry I'm late! I got held up! I didn't mean to . . .' she slows down, calms. I hope it is because she sees the relief reflected in my eyes. 'Thank you for waiting.'

'I was worried,' I admit. 'But I wanted to see you. More than anything.'

She smiles, and this time it is a quiet smile that I believe is meant for only me. She holds out a palm and nods towards the heart of the orchard. 'Shall we walk?'

Nerves quiver the tips of my fingers. I slip my hand in hers. 'I'd like that.'

Prey

I am soaring over the hills on my way home. This must be what true flying feels like. Not the lurching, stomach-tumbling thrill of being carried while a mother's wings beat down the air around you. I am gliding on thermals of joy, plunging headfirst into free-wheeling triumph and celebration.

Dusk draws in while I run the faint mountain trails. My hair bounces against my back; it feels heavier, gathered into a single plait braided by Yolanthe. She added a yellow ribbon and a purple flower from the orchard.

'Our secret,' we agreed. I will tell Mum I found these treasures. She can bear the weight of a ribbon for our next flight.

Even as I think it, I push the thought away. So bittersweet, this happiness.

'Must you leave?' Yolanthe had asked me again.

'Yes,' I said simply. I would not forsake my only family. As best I could, I tried to explain why.

She only had more questions. 'You're an orphan? So your mum adopted you? Do you know what happened to your real parents?'

'I never knew them,' I told her. 'Mum found me in a cardboard box that was left on a hillside where goats graze. She has cared for me ever since.'

'That's awful.'

'I don't think so.'

'I meant about being abandoned.'

The sadness in her face made me uncomfortable. 'Mum is kind. She tries her best, though she doesn't always understand.'

'My parents are like that,' Yolanthe replied quietly. Her hand squeezed mine. 'I don't think they'd understand.'

For many moments, we sat in the shade of the mouldering wall, leaning against each other. She wore another of those frilly shirts that folded down around her upper arms. I wished I wore a similarly scant piece of clothing, so I might feel her skin against mine. Shoulder to shoulder. But it was enough, and I will hold it all in my heart for the rest of my life.

I learned that Yolanthe likes to paint, and she plays the flute, and she takes her younger brother to play football on the weekends before working at the ice cream stand. She has climbed all of the nearest hills surrounding her hometown. She longs to go further. She is aching to leave her nest and fly. Yolanthe sells ice cream in the little square because it is her uncle's business and her family wishes to keep her close while she builds her wings, but already she yearns to soar into the sky and cross continents, leaving them all behind.

The light fades while I walk, and I must be more careful in picking my way across the mountainside. Though I know the way well, it is still possible to get turned around under the trees, and the last slice of moon is not yet high enough to guide me.

Small, black shapes flit between openings in the branches. Bats. Moths. Winged night creatures, brought alive by the dark. Mum will be waking up now. I hope she does not worry.

I follow the trickling sound of the stream until it leads me into a more open space, and I can see the first stars pricking the night sky. A large shadow passes overhead. It is followed by a hawkish scream.

I crouch out of instinct. Thorns graze my knees. My neck cranes up, tracking the shape circling in the sky above me.

It is familiar, and yet unknown.

It has the broad, feathered wings and long streaming hair of my mother. But, unlike her, this one has symmetrical wings and perfect, tapered tail feathers. The talons are invisible against its shadowed outline, but they are almost certainly tucked tight against the body.

The creature circles as she would, eyeing up prey before a kill.

I am only yards away from the tree line.

I begin to run.

The beast lets out another high-pitched caw. An unmistakeable hunting cry.

The bottom drops out of my stomach as I hear answering calls resound through the air: three distinct voices. The flap of many wings becomes a drum beat overhead.

A rush of air sweeps across my back as I dive under dense branches. I risk thorns for the protection they might provide. Barely silhouetted against an almost moonless sky, I track the shapes that circle and swoop above.

Another plunges down. I shrink into a hollow in the ground. Talons snatch at brambles, inches from my face. Broken branches rain down around me as the hissing monster tears back up again. I don't know whether to run again or lie still. My muscles make the choice for me, having seized stiff with fear.

The sounds change. They are all descending. More slowly this time. One lands in a tree. Another on the ground. The last one rattles the branches of my bush with a wing.

My senses are too dull. Now the harpies have muted their caws, they may as well be invisible in the dark. I strain to pick out the shuffling movements of the two on the ground. A rancid odour betrays just how close they are. The smell of rotting meat on their breath – a warm gust hits my ear. Peeking between fingers, all I see is a patch of slightly less-dark sky above me, illuminated only by the twinkling of stars.

The stars blink out. Another shadow passing overhead.

A screech pierces the night. Mum's voice. My heart leaps. I hear the frantic rustle of feathers as the other harpies crane their necks upwards, and Mum comes crashing down on top of them. Branches explode by my head as a feathered body is ripped away from me. I don't see the blood, but I hear the tearing of flesh, feel droplets hit my skin. I cover my face with my arms, curl into a tight ball while a frenzied struggle hurls around me.

One of the foreign voices shrieks, '*Traitor-Sissssssster!*'

It is cut off by a wet hacking noise. More flapping of wings, the snapping of my mother's angry caws. Trees creak as bodies launch through the canopy, tearing out into open sky. The beating of wings becomes distant. There is only the ragged wheezing of my mother left.

Slowly, I unfurl. 'Mum?' I whisper.

She is a gaunt shape in the dim starlight. Shoulders hunched, wings drooping to the ground. I approach, cautiously. My feet kick through loose feathers. I reach out a trembling hand to touch her. It comes away wet and sticky.

'Not ssssssafe,' she hisses.

'We need to get back to the nest,' I say, fighting back the tremor in my voice.

She lets me closer, allows me to lend my shoulder for support. Tears tumble down my cheeks as I carry her, achingly slow, along the trail. I am scared to leave the trees again, but we must cross the glade to reach our home.

My eyes remain trained on the sky as we walk. Mum stumbles, graceless in her steps and relying heavily on me to guide her. She is very light – I am almost fearful of breaking her.

Hours, it seems, for us to reach the hidden sanctuary of our nest. She eases painfully inside, wings dragging against rock and twigs.

I hurriedly switch on my little lights. Then, with a squeak of fear, I think to use one of my blankets to cover the opening of the nest, so that none will see the light from outside.

Mum folds up, wings drawn over her head. Her breathing is laboured, shallow. In the light I can now see the deep, bloody gashes, feathers torn from their roots. She shies away from my touch.

'Let me see,' I murmur. 'Mum, let me see so I can help you.'

She shudders, but lifts a wing. More ugly lacerations criss-crossing her skin, a clear talon-swipe across her pale breasts. I bring water and the cleanest of my blankets, and strive to rinse the wound before applying pressure to it. I don't know much of what to do in this situation, but on the radio plays sometimes there is a story of a murder, or a dramatic accident, and they always talk of applying pressure to the wound. I know there should be bandages and maybe medicines to fight an infection.

Mum had an infected foot once before – a goat's horn that broke the skin when she grabbed it, and a stone got wedged inside. I cleaned her talons then, removed the stone. Stole bandages from the village. It was only a small cut, but she had limped for weeks and we went hungry until it healed.

Now, I do my best to wrap blankets about her chest. Blood still oozes, but more slowly than before. Her eyelids flutter between open and closed.

I can't let her stay like this.

'I'm going back to the town, Mum,' I whisper. 'For things to heal you.'

I stroke hair from her forehead. Her skin is slick with sweat.

With a grunt, her yellow eyes focus on me briefly. 'No. Sssstay. Not sssssafe.'

'I'll wait until dawn. I'll be fast.' Knots tighten in my chest. 'Why did they attack me, Mum? You never hunt people.'

Her hand, quivering with the effort, touches my cheek. 'Aaaaangry. Chase us. Hunt youuuu.'

'They're chasing us?' I don't know if I've heard her right. 'Do you know them?'

'Sissssssters.'

'Why are they angry? What have we done?'

She blinks slowly. Her hand falls away. 'My child,' she says, in a whistling breath. '*Mine.*'

I begin to understand. Crows will attack outsiders to the flock. The lammergeier will not tolerate others in its territory. Or maybe they consider me a cuckoo, a trickster invading my mother's nest.

It conjures a darkness in me. We have always been running. Always moving. I have always assumed it was people we were fleeing from. Not family.

I've never encountered another harpy besides my mother before. We live in seclusion. But she has sisters, who would tear her to shreds like this?

And they are the reason I was to be torn from

Yolanthe. The reason we can never sit still, live in true peace. I wish to build a nest and keep it. Now I understand why we never have.

I press my forehead to Mum's, absorb the heat there. I feel the quivering of her whole body. A snarl rises from my belly. I feel ferocious.

'They will not hurt you again,' I swear.

I sit with Mum until she sleeps, singing half-remembered songs from the radio to soothe her. When she finally sinks into slumber, I steel myself for the journey ahead.

Though my muscles are tired and my heart is heavy, a fire burns deep in my core. I click off the lights and slip quietly from the nest.

Carrion

After a fretful, stumbling journey through the dark, I arrive at the edge of town and rest briefly in the old orchard while dawn blooms over the hillsides. I put the dull ache of blisters out of my mind and focus on my plan. The people will be opening their shops soon. Waiting for open doors shall be easier than trying to break in.

I skulk through the narrow streets. People stop on their doorsteps to stare at me, and I hurry quickly by. My appearance is likely more ragged than usual. Too late, I realise my clothes are covered in bloodstains. I fold my arms and hunch my shoulders, willing invisible wings around my-self. But I needn't have worried too much – when town people spy something that may interrupt their own agenda, they are more likely to avoid it. Several men duck their heads as they walk past me. One harried mother mutters, 'I've no change,' thinking that I approach her.

I turn the corner to the pharmacy and slink inside. I must be quick. It is the same woman behind the counter who chased me out before. Hopefully, she has not seen me yet.

There is a shelf full of bandages. I stare blankly at them for a moment, then start grabbing one of everything.

Heels click against the tile floor. I drop plastic packets as I struggle to bundle it all into my satchel.

'It's you!' cries the woman, from the end of the aisle.

I freeze in place. For a long second she holds my gaze. Then I bolt – but she is prepared this time. Her hand catches my sleeve. I shriek and hiss, turn to lash out with my other arm . . .

She is holding out a packet of bandages. Her face is tight, mouth pulled in a tense line. But her eyes are warm and gentle.

'You dropped this,' she says softly, letting go of my sleeve.

I snatch the packet from her. Bounce from foot to foot, uncertain whether to take flight again.

I'm uncomfortable under her quiet scrutiny. She looks at me openly, sees the whole of me – like Yolanthe sees me.

'Are you hurt?' she asks.

I shake my head.

'Whose blood is that?'

'My mother's,' I whisper.

Her forehead crinkles. 'I can call for an ambulance.'

I shrink away, edging for the door. 'We can't do that.'

'Wait.' Her voice is so quiet. She holds out a hand, a gentle beckoning. As though she thinks I am a frightened deer, and she is trying so hard not to startle me. 'How badly is she hurt?'

My voice wobbles. 'It's bad. Really bad.'

The woman worries at her bottom lip as she stares at the packets in my arms. Then she reaches to the shelves, pulls down a bottle of liquid and presses it into my hands. 'Antiseptic. To clean around any wounds. Please, try to persuade her to come to the hospital. I'd even drive you–'

'I'll tell her,' I blurt through tears. 'Thank you.'

I feel the weight of her anxiety on my back as I leave. My legs move with haste, in case she changes her mind and calls someone to stop me – but no one does. The little blue café is my next stop. I have seen lit candles on their tables during previous visits. Flames flickering romantically between couples, beautiful people in soft clothes, heads inclined in soft conversation.

Now I arrive to find the candles snuffed out. The people inside are drowsy, blinking in the fresh daylight. I smell coffee and sugar when the door opens. A waiter spies me standing on the doorstep and I duck hurriedly out of sight.

But still, I think, there are candles on the tables. That means matches, somewhere.

'Iphis?'

My lungs seize. I should be thrilled to hear her voice. Any other time. Not here. Not now.

I keep myself turned away. 'Hello, Yolanthe.'

She swings in front of me. The hem of a yellow sundress flaps about her knees. Numbly, I register how elegant her legs are, the daintiness of her sandaled feet.

'I thought you'd left town.' Faint irritation laces

her words, but quickly melts to concern. 'Are you okay?'

Her hand touches my arm, then pulls back abruptly. She stares at the state of my tunic. 'What happened to you?'

I daren't look at her. I know that if I do, I won't be able to keep from telling her everything. I clutch the strap of my satchel tightly and stay silent, head pointed at the ground.

Yolanthe's hands clasp my shoulders. Such warmth emanating from them. She pulls close, willing me to meet her stare. I must say something.

'I was attacked,' I say feebly. Yolanthe draws a sharp breath.

'Where? By who? Are you hurt?' Her eyes land on the first aid packets poking out the top of my bag.

'In the hills,' I reply, carefully ignoring half her questions. 'On my way home. I have to get back . . .'

'Alone?' There's an unfamiliar note of incredulity in her voice, a sharpness so close to anger that I'm momentarily startled.

She's quick to mark my deer-spooked expression. Her grip tightens on my shoulders. 'I'm going to walk you home, Iphis. I don't care how far it is.'

I stare blankly at her flimsy sandals. How easy it would be to tear the skin. A single thorn bush – or a talon swipe. 'It's dangerous.'

She presses her forehead to mine. 'Then I'm *definitely* not letting you go alone.'

* * *

I follow Yolanthe in a daze to her parents' house. Her father is visiting friends, she says, and her mother is delivering cakes to the little blue café. She invites me inside. I tiptoe over the threshold.

I have never been inside a people nest before. I have only stared longingly through back windows, rooted through the garbage that comes out of them.

Yolanthe's house has white stone walls and cool marble tiles. The curtains and the rugs are royal blue – somehow bluer than the sky. There are yellow patterned vases and sumptuous velvet cushions. And photos on every wall; Yolanthe smiles at me from many angles. Her family smiles, too.

I know I am a trespasser in this world.

Yolanthe guides me down a wide hallway to her bedroom. She opens a door and I'm greeted by a new rainbow of colour. A painting of a brilliant crimson sunset over a mountain range takes up most of one wall. An open easel in the middle of the room supports a white canvas; it bears the faint traces of a feminine figure drawn in pencil. The mat beneath is splattered with paint. There are sequins and tassels on the bedspread. She keeps violet flowers in a jar by her desk.

My gaze darts about the room, absorbing everything, burning it into my memory. Yolanthe's room. Yolanthe's life.

She slides open a smooth door in the wall, reveals a vibrant line of hanging clothes.

'Try this on,' she tells me, selecting one.

It is a deep, rich purple. A long dress that billows in the sleeves and cuts an exposing vee from my neck to the top of my chest. She turns away as I change. The fabric is silky soft against my skin. When she looks again, she catches me running the hem through my fingers.

'It looks good on you,' she says. Her eyes linger.

'We need to hurry,' I reply, bashfully tucking errant strands of hair behind one ear.

She pulls on shorts under her dress and swaps sandals for thick walking boots. A small backpack she fills with bottled water and trail snacks from her desk drawers. 'I'm ready.'

I hesitate before making a request. It shouldn't be this easy. 'I . . . need some matches. To start a fire.'

Yolanthe scratches her head, but ultimately shrugs. 'There's a box in the kitchen.' She grabs it on our way out – I get a glimpse of shining silver worksurfaces and more marbled stone – and strides with purpose to the door. 'Where do you live? Shall I drive us there?'

I shake my head. 'No roads go to it.'

We step into the street, Yolanthe matching my earnest pace to the edge of town. 'Just how far out is it?'

'Half a day's walk.'

'Have you ever considered getting a bike?' she suggests lightly. She bounces next to me, head high, as we walk through the cobbled avenues of her home. People smile at her, and she smiles back.

'Mum would never be able to carry it . . .' I falter, registering puzzlement in her expression.

At the orchard, I stop short. Dappled sunlight dances over us as I wring the front of the dress through my hands.

'You shouldn't come with me, Yolanthe.' I announce it so fast that the words blur together. 'I don't think you'll believe me if I told you why. But I don't want you to get hurt. I really, *really* don't want you to get hurt.'

For a split-second she looks as though she'll crack a joke, but then her mouth settles into a sombre frown. 'If you try to leave me behind, I'm only going to follow you.'

She laces her fingers in mine. My throat has closed up; I can barely breathe. I am so used to doing everything alone.

'This way,' I say, looking at the ground.

She walks by my side, no longer bouncing. Her mood changes, grows heavier the further we travel. I feel as though she is absorbing the tension from me, allowing me to be a little lighter, a little faster than my tired legs would otherwise go.

The sun beats down on us, beading sweat on Yolanthe's skin. She hitches up her dress as we traverse thicker foliage, emerge onto bare hillside of dry yellow grass. I show her the babbling stream, where we cool our feet for five minutes' rest.

'You really walk this far every day?' she asks me.

'Not every day,' I reply. Our shadows are stretching, and I am afraid of what the dusk might bring. 'We need to keep moving. It will be dark soon.'

I note the way her eyes dart into shadows as we continue. She jumps at a nearby rustle of grass. Just a sheep.

She reaches for my hand again. 'Is this where you were attacked?'

'Close.'

'I should have left a note for my parents.' She smiles nervously. Her hand is clammy. 'My phone doesn't have any signal out here.'

'We are nearly at my home.'

Yolanthe's anxiety seems to grow as we enter the covered dell where my nest is hidden. She hugs close to me with each step.

'We're here,' I say. When I point to the dark hole under the rock, her face is a mask of confusion.

'In there?' she asks uncertainly.

I dip my head in and pull aside the swathe of cloth covering the entrance. 'I'll go first. It's important that you stay behind me.'

On hands and knees, she follows me inside. Hands crunch softly down onto twigs and feather fluff. I reach for my fairy lights and flick them on.

Yolanthe gasps. I hear her voice hitch, draw into a squeal–

I turn and hug her tightly, muffling her scream into my shoulder. 'It's all right,' I say. 'It's all right. It's all right.'

'What *is* that?'

The sound of rustling behind me. I let go of Yolanthe so I am ready to block my mother – but I've forgotten how weak she is. She merely stares at us both from the floor of the nest. Her yellow eyes wink erratically, pupils shrinking and dilating. Perhaps she cannot focus.

I kneel, lift up her wing so I can reach her chest. Yolanthe gasps again. She seems frozen yet engrossed, tracking the sweep of smooth skin from Mum's jaw to her collarbone. Over the swell of her round breasts, from which the first downy feathers sprout, and then merge into longer, darker feathers over the rest of her torso. They flow over the line of her hip, which folds more acutely than a human hip, and one long, scaled leg juts out at an awkward angle, talons grasping the nest out of pain and fear.

'This is my mother,' I say.

'Your *what?*'

Yolanthe collapses, shuffling to the farthest edge of the nest. She hugs her knees and watches me mutely.

I touch the strips of fabric I'd previously used to bind Mum's wounds. Mum flinches away, hisses at me. I narrowly evade a swipe of talons.

'I'm going to help you,' I tell her calmly.

I begin by unwrapping one of the long bandages. My first task is to bind her legs. I coax the other leg out from its folded position, and strap them tightly together so she can't swipe at me again. She doesn't have the strength to fight me, anyway.

'You can't be serious,' I hear Yolanthe murmur. 'This thing isn't your mum.'

'She saved me,' I say, while I begin to clean around the broken flesh with antiseptic. 'She could have left me to die on the mountain, but she didn't.'

Warm breath tickles my shoulder. Yolanthe peers down, eyes wide with morbid curiosity. 'Is she safe?'

'No.'

She glances at the talons. 'I meant–'

'I know what you meant. She's very dangerous. But not often to people. We steer clear of you, as much as we can.' I place a swatch of gauze over the open gash and wind another bandage to secure it in place.

'She looks like a monster.'

'She's not.' I meet Yolanthe's gaze. She recoils – perhaps my expression is too fierce. I wonder how I look to her now, in this dim light, tending to my monstrous mother in the purple dress she has lent me.

I make an effort to dowse any fury that might lace my voice; to soften my face into something kinder. 'We are just surviving. We hide from people to keep ourselves safe. She means no harm to anyone.'

Yolanthe seems pensive. Her stare bores into me. 'You care about her very much.'

'Yes.'

'I've always thought...' Tentatively, she

touches my wrist. 'It seemed like you were running from something.'

The little bird is back in my chest, fluttering eagerly, if a little wearily. 'I was. We were.'

Yolanthe's fingers brush the very tips of Mum's flight feathers. 'Was it people who attacked her?'

'No.' Mum's eyes have drifted closed. I hope she is finding our voices soothing. 'It was her sisters.'

I feel the sudden stillness in Yolanthe's body. 'There are more of them?'

'At least three.'

'Why do they want to hurt you?'

I gaze at Mum's feeble form. My heart is heavy. 'I suppose they're not pleased she took me in. I'm not like them.'

I stroke Mum's cheek. She is unconscious again. I hope I've done enough.

Yolanthe's arms hug my waist. Her cheek feels wet against my neck.

'Come and live with me,' she says. 'This is madness, Iphis! You don't have to live out here, in the dirt.'

I pry her hands carefully away. 'I'm not going to leave her.'

'But what if the others . . . her sisters . . . what

if they come back? Will they attack you again? You can't *stay* here, Iphis,' she pleads.

'You don't understand.' I twist so I can sit facing her. There is an edge to my voice that frightens even me. 'I'm not going to let them hurt her again, Yolanthe.'

Yolanthe's eyes flick from Mum to me. Her bottom lip trembles.

But she swallows. Her fists clench. 'What do we need to do?'

The darkness swirling in my chest is uplifted as her steady gaze mirrors mine. I pull the matches from my bag. 'Set a trap.'

Predator

The night crowds in over my head, hushed and heavy. I sit in the open glade, not far from the nest. A small campfire is prepared in front of me, unlit. My back is straight, hands mindlessly winding my radio while I watch the sky. I don't care whether they return this night, or the next. I will be waiting here.

But I am certain they will come tonight. It is the moonless sky. The perfect time for a harpy to travel.

Even though my eyes are well-adjusted to the dark, I struggle to pick out clear shapes in this starlit shadow-world. The first warning of their approach is a leaden flap of wings.

I slip the strap of the radio around my wrist. It knocks awkwardly against my elbow while I scrabble for matches. The rhythm of thumping air increases in tempo. I strike the match – it sparks but the end snaps off. Desperately, I grab another.

Three rasps against the box before it ignites. I hold the flame to wadded newspaper and dried grass. Red embers flicker before the flame dies. Perspiration glazes my brow as I try the third match. Hunting shrieks rain down on me as I produce another tiny flame. Sheltered by my shaking hands, it licks at the tinder offerings.

Finally – it catches! Just in time. The first of the plunging harpies swerves last-second, repelled by the sudden flare of fire. I seize my radio and turn the volume to its highest. The chortling voices of my favourite talk show hosts blare across the hillside. In the dim glow of the growing campfire, I see the dark shapes of the harpies circling over me. The noise seems to have had the desired effect. They don't know what to make of the multitude of human voices. It has bought me time.

I pick up the makeshift torch I'd prepared earlier: a long branch with a dense spray of small twigs wrapped tightly in bandages at one end. It crackles and pops as I hold it in the fire.

A harpy dives. She is enormous compared

to my mother. I brandish the torch in an arc over my head, shedding a stream of glowing cinders through the air. The harpy screeches, ragged wings striving to twist her trajectory mid-air. I catch a flash of green in her golden eyes, a trace of wrinkles in her pallid face.

She doesn't back off like I expect, but rather comes in for another approach. I hold my torch out at the ready, radio still blaring from my wrist. But the harpy dodges me and sweeps for the camp-fire. She lands and– *whoompf.* One wing smothers the entire fire in a deliberate, heavy movement.

She glowers, half-crouched on the ground. In my flickering torchlight, I see her features clearly. She looks like my mum, with the same petite nose and pointed cheekbones. But much, much older, with deep crow's feet at her eyes and loose skin around her jaw.

She caws – a signal. The two circling harpies plummet. I've already started sprinting.

I hold the torch out behind me as I run, blindly swiping up and down. I feel it make contact, a brief hiss as the harpy pulls back her talons. A thump as her sister veers and crashes into the ground.

More pulsing wingbeats suggest the older harpy has returned to the air.

I slide into the thicket, knowing the branches will slow them down. I keep the torch high: my position prominent. The sound of crunching leaves and chittering calls alerts me to their progress. They are keeping pace with me. Good.

The overhanging rock looms in the darkness. A talon snatches my dress – I tear free and vault into the hole. I hit the floor of our nest face first, grazing my right shoulder. But I've kept the torch aloft.

I scramble to the furthest corner. The nest dips in this spot, where Mum and I have spent most of our time, and I can stand tall without hitting my head on the rock ceiling.

For the harpies, it's not so easy. They come tumbling into the nest, getting tangled in each other's wings and claws. The oldest harpy is first to rise, rearing on her haunches, but hunched under the cramped confines. She hobbles forward, hissing at the sparks from my torch as I wave it in front of her face.

'Where issssss sheeeee?' she spits from between bared teeth.

'Mum is safe,' I declare. 'I won't let you find her.'

'No daughter, are youuuuu,' she replies, mangling vowels from a throat clearly unaccustomed to human-speech.

'It's her choice,' I say, standing my ground. 'And mine.'

I pitch the torch to one side. The harpy's eyes follow the sputtering flames – then widen as she sees them lick at a heap of bundled newspapers. The flames leap onto them.

Suddenly our hole is brightly lit. Fire races along the edges of the nest. The newspaper is arranged in twists, stacked next to each other along the lip of the nest, each one catching fast. Woven among them are strips of my linen tunic and dried grass. Crackling hazel brushwood balances on top. We are surrounded, entrapped by a blazing wall of fire.

The harpies panic. The two younger sisters scream as though they are dying; one scrabbles at the rock above while the other tries to dig a way out through the bottom. The older harpy also shrieks, then makes to lunge at me. But I am turning the dial on my radio, and now I blast disorienting, buzzing white noise at its highest volume.

She falls backwards, eyes rolling back into her head with terror.

I am shaking. The heat on my face is intense; I can taste smoke in my mouth. But adrenaline thuds along my arteries, and I am fuelled as much by anger as I am by fear.

'*Leave!*' I roar at them. 'Leave us alone! I have fire, and I have demon sounds! And if you come near us again, *I will make you pay!*'

I take a step towards the lead harpy. She's fallen back onto her wings, pawing awkwardly at the air with her talons like a turtle. She shrinks under my advance, scraping at the nest with her elbows to shuffle away.

A strange noise rises from her throat. A keening, wailing sort of sound.

'*Daughter.*' It's a grief-filled cry. Tears flood the harpy's cheeks. '*Give baaaaack daughter.*'

Woozy in the oxygen-starved haze, I struggle to make sense of this. 'Leave us alone,' I repeat.

I am still holding my torch, now a dazzling firebrand which is nearly scorching my fist. I jab it at her chest, smell the charcoal-like odour of burned flesh and feathers. '*I will hunt you,*' I snarl. '*Do you understand?*'

My eyes are streaming from the smoke, but I force them open. See the rictus of dread on the harpy's face.

She turns and gathers the other two under her broad wings, pushing them all to the small opening. I hear the younger ones spluttering, mewling, as they gracelessly lurch out into the clean night air.

Before she follows them, the elder turns to look at me one last time through the fumes. Her green-yellow eyes narrow. '*Monster,*' she hisses.

Then, in a whisper of feathers, she is gone.

I sway on the spot. I have dropped my torch. Dimly, I note that a pattern of flames is forming across the floor of the nest. The hairs on my arms are singed.

I drop to my knees. It pulls my head out of the cloud of smoke rising to the roof, and I inhale a few relatively cleaner lungfuls of oxygen. But I'm very light-headed, and as I crawl forward I'm no longer sure whether I'm going in the right direction to escape the nest.

My vision whirls in yellows and reds. Acrid fumes fill my mouth.

A dark shape rises in front of me. I'm enveloped by something black and soft, like feathers.

'Mum?' I sigh, as the shambling figure hauls me out of the nest.

We topple together onto the grass. It is like plunging into a pool of cool water. I roll onto my back, mouth lolling open, lapping up the air with my tongue.

My head is lifted, cradled in the crook of soft arms. Gentle hands spill water across my face, let it drip between my lips.

Gradually the stars swim into focus above me. Someone is stroking my hair. I tip my head back and meet Yolanthe's troubled gaze.

I smile.

'They're gone,' I croak.

She nods. Kisses my forehead. Around her shoulders, I register the soft, charred remnants of one of my blankets.

'I left your Mum sleeping,' she says. 'She's safe.'

'Thank you.'

I doze for a moment, watching the stars.

'That was really brave,' Yolanthe whispers against my hair. 'Do you think they'll attack again?'

I turn my head, concealing the sadness that suddenly threatens to wash over me. 'No. I don't think they want to hurt Mum.' My voice is hoarse. 'I think perhaps they were trying to save her. From me.'

Yolanthe's hands halt their stroking. 'That's nonsense. You're her *daughter,* Iphis.' Her forehead meets mine. 'And after everything you've told me, I'm certain she'll always choose to be your mum.'

I lean up and capture her lips in a kiss. Her fingers clench in my hair, then slide down over my shoulders, wrapping me in a ferocious hug. I curl into her chest, resting my face against her neck.

We stay like this for a long time. Until the fire is out, and dawn beckons on the horizon.

Nesting

Yolanthe and I are hiking.

Our feet squelch over moist sheep tracks, mud caking our boots while a light drizzle of rain lifts the sweat from our cheeks. The air is fresh and fragrant with the smell of fallen leaves.

Winter is always lovely here. Mum and I used to migrate far south, chasing the warm weather. She feared the cold. But I find it's never really too cold on the lower hills, and I enjoy the changing character of our rippling mountain valley.

These hills are home.

It's been nearly ten years since I last migrated with Mum. Ten years since we last ran away from anything. Now I run forever forwards, with Yolanthe by my side.

I've travelled more in the last decade of my life

than I ever did in the first two. Together, Yolanthe and I explored the ancient, throbbing heart of Athens; got lost in a crowd of tourists at the Parthenon. In museums we found pictures of harpies on Attic pottery. In libraries we found the stories. I told Yolanthe it was unfair that Mum should be lumped in with these vengeful servants of myth: the winged hounds of Zeus.

In an act of defiance, we conquered Mount Olympus together. Shouted obscenities at the god of thunder in the sky. Laughed together, on the way back down.

Yolanthe taught me how to swim in the warm waters of the Aegean Sea. I taught her how to recognise edible Horta everywhere we travelled – we picked wild amaranth and dandelions, cooked with mountain sage and rock samphire.

We saw wonders together. From the thumping port metropolis of Thessaloniki to the silent and pristine waters of the Great Prespa Lake . . . from the quietest forgotten hillside shrines to the bustling Minoan palace at Knossos. I learned how to make money giving hiking tours to people who wanted to flee their nests and be wild for a while. We scraped a living while teaching others how to scrape the land. I joined Yolanthe's world and discovered how to invite her into mine.

Always, we returned home. To these rocky slopes, south of a familiar mountain I learned was named Parnassus. We know the treasures of these steep ravines and rolling foothills best of all. But we give no tours here. This is our space, alone.

In the distance, the highest peaks are dusted with snow. Low-hanging clouds mute the sun's rays. Still, we are warm with the exertion.

Yolanthe stops to adjust the straps on her baby-carrier.

'Do you want me to take her for a while?' I offer.

She quirks her lips. 'You can do the way back.' She rolls her shoulders, then strains to peer underneath her own chin. 'Does she look okay? Comfortable?'

I check Yolanthe's precious cargo. Curled against her chest, partially hidden under a pink bobble hat, and a fat cheek smooshed adorably against Yolanthe's fuzzy jumper, our baby girl snores peacefully. I stroke a strand of brown curly hair away from her eyes. 'She looks perfect.'

We continue our trek. I'm pleased to see the

trail appears undisturbed, save for occasional rabbit droppings.

Descending into a wet gorge, with tree branches dripping over our heads, we wind our way towards a sheltered clearing. Impossible to see from the hillside, we only spot the hollow when we are on top of it – and mainly because of the slightly conical pile of flat stones that form a roof, poking into view.

Its grey, circular shape is a welcome sight. Once, in centuries past, these dry-stone walls were used as a shepherd's hut. A waypoint for a wandering lifestyle, tending to a roaming flock. But shepherds now steer their sheep away from these hills, having lost too many to the steep drops and jagged rocks.

We duck hastily inside, eager to be out of the rain. We chuckle as we shake raindrops from our coats as though ruffling feathers. I reach for the solar-powered lantern that hangs from a hook in the ceiling. It fills the space with warm yellow light.

'It's us, Mum,' I say to the dark shape furled against the wall. 'We've brought someone special to meet you, today.'

Her feathers shiver as she unfolds. The broken wing still gives her pain, especially in these colder months. I feel a pang of guilt that it never healed properly. But she is burrowed in a nest of warm blankets that has grown steadily over the years: a fortress of cashmere, velvet, and silk. This time I have brought a merino wool sweater to add to the pile.

Mum's eyes open, blink lazily at us. 'Issssss foood?' she drawls.

I open my backpack, begin stacking tupperware on the ground. 'Would you like fish, or chicken, or lamb today?'

'Fiiiiiish,' she replies pleasantly.

I crack open the tub, allow her to snatch it from me. She eats with the greediness of an en-thusiastic appetite, rather than of fraught hunger. She always enjoys the food we bring. Yolanthe is a wonderful cook, and even I have learned how to do more with my meat than merely burn it.

Yolanthe unbuckles the carrier. She passes me the child, who is just beginning to wake, while she digs out a bottle of prepared formula. The baby cries, a whine of hunger and general discomfort with the world at large. Mum looks up. Her pupils contract, training on the squirming infant.

I step closer, kneel so she can get a better look. 'Mum. Meet your grand-daughter.'

Yolanthe's hand clasps my shoulder. 'Her name is Aello.'

Mum's head tips to one side. Measuring. Appraising.

'She's like me,' I explain tenderly, fondling Aello's fluffy booted toes. 'She was abandoned by her real parents. So, we're her parents, now. We chose. Like you did.'

I lift my eyes to Mum's. She is still staring past me. Aello's cry burgeons into a wail.

Mum sniffs the air. Leans forward, nostrils flaring. Her talon dips into the tupperware, hooks out a sliver of glistening fish. She proffers it to the writhing babe in my arms.

'Foooood,' she says, so softly.

Yolanthe's hand relaxes. She joins me on the floor, and together we feed our daughter from the bottle. Mum watches while humming a soothing tone, almost like a purr, deep in her throat. The crying ceases, replaced by the contented suckling of the child.

Mum shifts closer, shuffling her crippled wings over the floor. She dips her left wing, so that one of the ragged feathers tickles Aello's nose.

The baby pauses in her nursing. Giggles.

Time stands still within a perfect moment.

I look down.

Aello is smiling at me.

About the Author

Georgina Jeffery is a British author of speculative fiction. Her stories often blend elements of fantasy, humour, and horror, and tend to reflect her fascination with folklore from around the world. You'll find mythical beasties, malevolent spirits, and eldritch magic in a lot of her writing.

Georgina's work can be found in a variety of anthologies and journals, including *The NoSleep Podcast*, *Sci-Fi Lampoon*, *Unbreakable Ink*, *The San Cicaro Experience*, and *Copperfield Review Quarterly*.

ALSO BY GEORGINA JEFFERY

The Jack Hansard Series: Season One

Funny urban fantasy with a lot of British folklore. Jack Hansard, occult salesman, turns reluctant detective when his merchandise is stolen and becomes embroiled in a supernatural kidnapping case.

The Jack Hansard Series: Season Two

Jack Hansard and his coblyn friend Ang are back in business. Together they face shapeshifters, piskies, and ancient magics in their quest to track down Ang's missing kin and uncover the secrets of Baines & Grayle.

Beyond Thundering Waters (Dark Folklore)

A dark fairy tale in a modern Norwegian setting. When a young girl meets a huldra in the Norwegian wilderness, she unwittingly makes a supernatural bargain that puts her Pappa's life at stake.

Within Trembling Caverns (Dark Folklore)

A dark fairy tale in a modern Polish setting. A grandmother cares for an ailing dragon . . . but her compassion places her own family in the jaws of danger.

Across Screaming Seas (Dark Folklore)

A dark fairy tale in a modern Welsh setting. A diver finds herself trapped in a mermaid's lair, wrestling against her own conscience and the need to survive.

Among Strangling Roots (Dark Folklore)

A dark fairy tale in a modern German setting. After inheriting her mother's dilapidated farm, Marion suffers nightmare visions and a monster from old nursery tales that stalks her daughter in the fields.